I0772843

"Yes I can"
and
The Book of I Am

By
DJ PHILLIPS

COPYRIGHTS

ISBN: 978-1963239461 (Paperback)

Published by American Book Publisher

For inquiries,

Email: info@americanbookpublisher.com

Phone: (929)-563-6133

Website: www.americanbookpublisher.com

ACKNOWLEDGMENT

I would like to first and foremost thank the Almighty Divine Creator, God, Mind, and Light of the Universe. I am not a religious man, and this is no cliché. The Almighty was there for me when nobody else was. The Almighty Divine heard me for the first time. It was myself, a flame by way of candle, Holy Divine Yeshu, and angel energy vibration, and from then we began a relationship for the first time.

I also want to acknowledge the publisher representatives of this book itself for also seeing my purpose and encouraging me on my soul mission and actually using the methods in this book themselves. Also, those number one people that have been sent into my life and have shared their own trials and encouragement to push forward with my dreams and soul purpose as I encourage them to keep pushing on. We all can't be fit into square holes; it's time for your true self to shine. No more low vibrations; sometimes it means making big choices to save one's soul.

I now refer to the most Holy Divine Creator as "I am"

AUTHOR BIO

Born and raised in the city of Toronto Ontario now a young fifty six years of age I was raised in your average family trying to get by but very comical at times that being said we all have our different personalities and have tried many things and deep inside I always knew I would be an author. Everything I write about will always be meant to inspire and spread a positive message and vibe.

Goodbye mom! I'm going to school
said Bobby

Goodbye Bobby have a nice day
said Bobby's mom

As he began his walk to
school.

On his walk to school,
Bobby's friend next door

Always waits for Bobby to join him to walk to school together.

One day Bobby noticed a very
colourful book among others put
out for trash by a neighbour on
thier way to school.

When Bobby brushed the dust off
the cover, the title read

" Yes I Can "
and
The Book of I Am

On the first page read

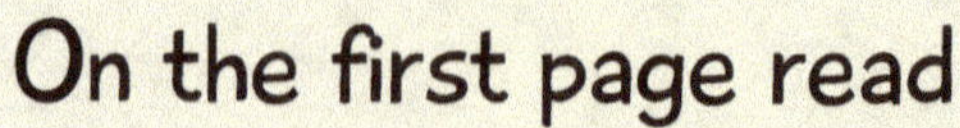

" In this book you will learn the super powers within your own self."

Bobby thought "cool" a
super hero book.

So soon the weekend came
and Bobby decided to start
reading his new book.

The first page had instructions to use the words "I am" after everytime you use your name, even if you write only your first name say the words "I am" after it in your mind so you will always remember to fill in the blank with your desired super power.

am Bobby ...Oh Bobby I am.......
ughhh an A student in math.

then say it two more times to equal
3 and do it daily every day, every
week, every month, every year, as
much as you can and make it a
normal part of your life and you have
to beleive you can do it because
now the magic energy needed has
started happening in the magic place
and you are the tool to make it
happen on earth.

Bobby thought
"hey this is pretty cool"

and in a deep super hero kind of voice
he murmered.
"I am Bobby, Bobby I am."

Chuckling after but Bobby I am with his new addition to his name vowed that he would follow the instructions.

So Bobby completed the first task and now it was time to turn the page and go onto the next set of instructions so Bobby turned the page...

to his surprise the next page was
blank so he turned the next page, then
another and another and to Bobby's
astonishment the rest of the book was
filled with blank pages.

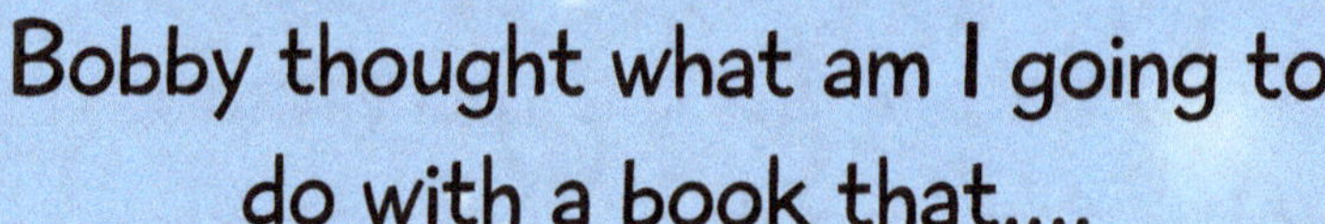

Bobby thought what am I going to
do with a book that....

wait he thought....what am I...........I
am......hmmm

what if.....hmm....Bobby's imagination started working as he thought to himeslf, " what if the I am after my name is to create the Super Bobby I always wanted to be?

Bobby sat in concentration as he started to say to himself three times

Bobby I am great at math,
Bobby I am great at math,
Bobby I am great at math.

Then Bobby would say,

Bobby I am winning the science fair,
Bobby I am winning the science fair,
Bobby I am winning the science fair,

and then
Bobby would say

Bobby I am grateful,
Bobby I am grateful,
Bobby I am grateful.

So days and weeks went by
as
Bobby made this his own fun
thing to continue doing
daily, nightly, weekly,
monthly

Bobby "I Am" recieving his sealed report card
from his teacher feeling confident.

until one day Bobby walked
home with the biggest most
beautiful trophy for winning
in the science fair and on top
of that handed his report
card to his mom to give her
the news.

As Bobby's mom read the report card and Bobby I am sat confident because of the instructions he was to follow Bobby I am's eyes lit up as his mom called out his grade in math. It was an A+

Oh my goodness
Bobby I am thought to himsellf,
I really did turn myself into my
own and super hero

Bobby's mom was even
astonished.

How did you do it Bobby?
his mom asked.

Bobby just smiled at his mom
and said

" That's Bobby I am" mom.

As he smiled and hugged his mom
he murmured to himself with a smile
and once more said...

"I am...Bobby I Am

www.ingramcontent.com/pod-product-compliance
Lightning Source LLC
Chambersburg PA
CBHW070357310726
48977CB00002B/481

9 781963 239461